WOMEN OF MYTHOLOGY
GODDESSES, WARRIORS, AND HUNTERS

MEDUSA

Jodyanne Benson

Cavendish
Square
New York

Published in 2020 by Cavendish Square Publishing, LLC
243 5th Avenue, Suite 136, New York, NY 10016

Library of Congress Cataloging-in-Publication Data

Names: Benson, Jodyanne, author.
Title: Medusa / Jodyanne Benson.
Description: First Edition. | New York : Cavendish Square, 2020. | Series:
Women of mythology: goddesses, warriors, and hunters | Includes bibliographical references and index.
Identifiers: LCCN 2019008834 (print) | LCCN 2019012797 (ebook) |
ISBN 9781502651433 (ebook) | ISBN 9781502651426 (library bound) |
ISBN 9781502651402 (pbk.) | ISBN 9781502651419 (6 pack)
Subjects: LCSH: Medusa (Greek mythology)--Juvenile literature.
Classification: LCC BL820.M38 (ebook) | LCC BL820.M38 B46 2020 (print) | DDC 398.20938/01--dc23
LC record available at https://lccn.loc.gov/2019008834

Editor: Kristen Susienka
Copy Editor: Alex Tessman
Associate Art Director: Alan Sliwinski
Designer: Christina Shults
Production Coordinator: Karol Szymczuk
Photo Research: J8 Media

Printed in the United States of America

TABLE OF CONTENTS

Swiss artist Arnold Böcklin painted this version of Medusa around 1878.

CHAPTER ONE

THE STORY OF THE SNAKE-HAIRED WOMAN

Scary. Shocking. Unforgettable. These words all describe Medusa. Her story has excited and scared readers for hundreds of years. Medusa is a special character. She doesn't stand for just one idea. She is a monster and beauty. She is a threat and protector. Let's learn more about how she became such an interesting character.

Medusa and Perseus

Medusa is a snake-haired monster. She appears in many Greek **myths**. Some of the myths have different details. However, the main story goes like this: Medusa and her two sisters were called the **Gorgons**. She was the only

This Greek statue of Perseus was created in the fourth century BCE.

mortal one. Some myths say that she was born a monster like her sisters. Later stories (like Ovid's) say that Medusa became a monster as a punishment from the goddess Athena. Anyone who looked at Medusa would turn into stone.

The hero Perseus, son of Zeus, was sent to kill Medusa. With help from the gods, he did. He was warned not to look directly at her. Instead, he gazed at her reflection in his shield. Led by her image in the mirror, he cut off her head.

Medusa and a god named Poseidon had two children. One child was Chrysaor. The other child was Pegasus. They were born the moment Medusa's head was cut off.

Athena used Medusa's face on her armor to protect her from enemies.

Perseus used Medusa's head for his own protection. He held it up to turn his enemies into stone. Perseus eventually gave Medusa's head to the goddess Athena. Athena put it on a shield to stop her enemies.

WRITERS AND MEDUSA

The Greek poet Hesiod lived between 750 and 650 BCE. The earliest version of Medusa's story is found in his poem called the *Theogony*. He explains the beginning part of her life and her death. Ovid's *Metamorphoses* gives more details about Medusa's story. Ovid was a Roman poet. He lived between 43 BCE and 17 CE.

This is a sketch of the Greek writer Hesiod.

Metamorphoses is a narrative poem. A narrative poem tells a story. It has characters and events just like in the stories you read. The word "metamorphoses" means **transformations**. Ovid's characters change throughout their lives. *Metamorphoses* includes over 250 Greek and Roman myths.

The Story's Message

The head of Medusa begins as an image of **chaos** and ugliness. As part of Athena's armor, it becomes something helpful. It gives Athena strength and protection. Even today, Medusa is not a simple character. She means different things to many different people.

Myth, Fable, or Folktale?

Myths are stories that make sense of the world. Fables are stories with animals who speak and act like people. Folktales are stories shared through word of mouth before there was writing.

ANOTHER STORY: BEOWULF

Beowulf is a heroic poem from England created between 700 and 750 CE. Like the story of Perseus, *Beowulf* is mythological. It is also a folktale. In the story, an evil monster named Grendel has been hurting King Hrothgar's warriors. Young Beowulf, a prince, defeats him. Then, Grendel's mother comes after Beowulf for killing her son. Beowulf also defeats Grendel's mother. The

This print from 1910 shows Beowulf attacking Grendel.

monsters in Beowulf stand for everything evil that cause fear. Beowulf becomes known as the example of goodness and light in the world.

Temples such as this one were built to honor gods and goddesses.

CHAPTER TWO

THE TRUTH BEHIND MYTHS

Think of something that scares you. Maybe it's thunderstorms. Maybe it's monsters living under your bed. The world can be a frightening place. What should we do when we're scared? How do we act bravely? Sometimes stories can help us be stronger.

People who lived in the **ancient** world were sometimes scared too. They asked themselves the same questions. They came up with myths to help them answer these questions.

The Importance of Myths

The Greeks are known for their myths of gods, goddesses, and heroes. The Greek myths were not written down like stories we read today. People told these stories to their friends and family over many years. The stories were remembered and eventually written down. They helped the Greeks understand their own lives. They taught important lessons like choosing good over evil.

The Olympian gods and goddesses ruled from Mount Olympus.

The stories were so important to the Greeks that they worshipped the gods. They even built temples to the gods.

Today, these stories are still very important. They continue to teach us about the world. As we get older, life brings more responsibility. This is where the story of the hero's quest can help us. Heroes teach us how to act in the face of things that scare us, like the dark. They show us how to be brave. They teach us how to make good choices.

In the story of Medusa, the hero Perseus has to face Medusa, a monster. Think of monsters as anything that makes us scared or uncertain. Perseus has a big assignment. He is unsure how to handle it. So, he asks for help from Athena. Sometimes gods and goddesses can be very helpful in

Muses and Music

The word "music" comes from the Muses. The Muses were goddesses of the arts in Greek mythology.

myths. They give people good advice. They help them overcome challenges.

Women and Mythology

Myths also shaped ancient culture. They tell us about what

The temple of Artemis shows Medusa in the center escaping Perseus (*right*).

people thought of women. Do you wonder why Medusa was a woman rather than a man? Women weren't necessarily seen as monsters, but they were seen as mysterious and unexplainable. Some women were so beautiful that it made men act differently

WOMEN AND POWER

This floor in Athens, Greece, shows Medusa's head in the center.

The main women in the myth of Medusa are very different. Medusa is a terrifying monster. Athena is a smart and courageous goddess. They are both powerful. Athena is admired, while Medusa is feared. Medusa's power is transformed by Athena. This makes sense because Athena is the goddess of wisdom, crafts, and war. These are all things that the Greeks, especially men, believed were good. Myths like Medusa's featured role models for the Greeks. Men looked to Perseus for his heroism, and Athena would have been a celebrated role model for women.

around them. This made men see women as very powerful people.

Women were important characters in myths. Some were helpful, but some caused problems. Athena, rather than Medusa, was a role model for women in the ancient world. Have you ever recognized parts of yourself in a character?

This jar is from the fourth century BCE. It shows Athena.

About the Theater

The ancient Greeks invented theater. Only men and boys were allowed to be actors. They wore masks that showed whether their character was happy or sad.

Medusa is a very popular character from Greek mythology. She can still be found in books, movies, and art today.

CHAPTER THREE
THE MODERN MEDUSA

Medusa is one of the most recognized characters in Greek mythology. Today, she is in books, movies, television shows, songs, comics, and video games. You can even order a spicy Medusa sushi roll from the menu at a Disney resort! If you look around, pictures of Medusa may be in more places than you think.

Medusa in Art and Culture

The painter Caravaggio's *Medusa* was created around 1598. Caravaggio created lifelike paintings. Caravaggio captured the moment that Medusa is beheaded. He was asked to make this piece as a gift for the Grand Duke of Tuscany. The painting

Caravaggio created this famous painting of Medusa in the sixteenth century.

decorates a wooden shield. The image is powerful on this tool of war. Caravaggio's version of Medusa doesn't look right at us. This makes her a little less scary to see.

For Perseus, Medusa was a monster to be destroyed. On Athena's shield, she became a powerful protector. Today, her reputation is complicated. She's a mysterious face that attracts people. Her name is also used to put down powerful women. In today's world, successful and powerful women are sometimes compared to Medusa. Their

Medusa Celebrated

Medusa is on the flag of Sicily and on the **coat of arms** of Dohalice, a village in the Czech Republic.

Fashion designer Versace used the face of Medusa for his logo. It is seen on this purse.

pictures have even been photoshopped to have snake hair. These women are seen as having too much power, and not everyone likes that.

However, the image of Medusa has

also been used in more positive ways. In the 1990s, Italian fashion designer Gianni Versace made the image of Medusa his personal **logo**. Her face was put on everything Versace made, like beautiful perfume bottles, scarves, and clothing. Versace believed that once people fell in love with his brand, they would love it forever.

Medusa Today

We've explored just a glimpse of Medusa through the ages. She's meant different things to different people. For the ancients, she was someone to fear. In recent history, her name still means "evil" to some people.

MEDUSA MEETS FAIRYTALES

Snow White from *Once Upon a Time* is a fierce character.

The television show *Once Upon a Time* featured the frightening Medusa. She had glowing red eyes and snake hair. In this retelling, Snow White and Prince Charming defeated her. Prince Charming tricked Medusa into coming out of her cave while Snow White waited to cut off her head. However, when Snow White tried to cut off Medusa's head, the sword shattered. So, Snow White used the reflective part of her shield and charged at Medusa with it. Medusa saw herself in the mirror and ended up turning herself into stone. *Once Upon a Time* made the ancient myth modern by making Snow White, a woman, the heroine.

Medusa has inspired the fashion world. This model wears a Medusa hairpiece for a hairdressing competition.

Some places have used her as a symbol of protection. They have decided to put her image on their flags. Despite these differences, we can be sure that Medusa is still an important character today.

Symbol and Art

The head of Medusa was seen as a symbol of protection. She is on Roman **mosaics** discovered in Pompeii.

GLOSSARY

ancient Old, or from a long time ago.

chaos Total confusion.

coat of arms Art that represents a family or a place.

Gorgons Three snake-haired sisters.

logo A symbol of a group or company.

mortal Able to die.

mosaics Pictures on a wall or floor with small colored tiles.

myths Stories that explain the world or a culture's beliefs.

transformations Changes over time.

FIND OUT MORE

Books

Flynn, Sarah Wassner. *Greek Mythology*.
Washington, DC: National Geographic, 2018.

Yasuda, Anita. *Explore Greek Myths!* White River
Junction, VT: Nomad Press, 2016.

Website

Who Were the Ancient Greek Gods and Heroes?

www.bbc.com/bitesize/articles/
zgt7mp3discover/history/greece/greek-gods

Video

Ancient Greece Facts for Kids

www.youtube.com/watch?v=wgvlzcPqPLU

INDEX

Page numbers in **boldface** refer to images. Entries in **boldface** are glossary terms.

ABOUT THE AUTHOR

Jodyanne Benson is a writer and editor from Wisconsin. A longtime teacher, Benson believes that great books spark wonder, curiosity, and learning. She enjoys reading and spending time with her family.